THERE'S A FUNGUS AMONG US

Your Complete Fungus-Growing Kit!

Originally published as *Grow Your Own Fungus*
By Carol Benanti
Illustrated by Andrew Crabtree
Cover illustration by Margaret A. Hartelius

Special thanks to Kathleen Kelly, Liberty Science Center, Jersey City, NJ.

Published in 1996 by Grosset & Dunlap, Inc., a member of The Putnam and Grosset Group, New York. BOOKS AND STUFF is a trademark of The Putnam & Grosset Group. GROSSET & DUNLAP is a trademark of Grosset & Dunlap, Inc. Originally published in 1995 by Pace Products, Inc. Published simultaneously in Canada.

Printed in the U.S.A.

ISBN 0-448-41344-2 A B C D E F G H I J

A World of Fungus

Fungi (the plural of fungus) live everywhere—in the air, in water, and on land. Fungi live underground, inside animals, on plants, and even in your shoes. Most fungi prefer warm, damp surroundings, so you'll find fungi all over the earth except where it is very cold or very dry. There is so much fungus in the world that there are scientists called *mycologists* who study nothing but fungi.

There are over 100,000 species of fungi, including tiny yeasts, giant rounded puffballs, slimy blobs, beautiful mushrooms, fluffy mildews, cobweb-like molds, and fungi that grow like shelves on trees. *There's a Fungus Among Us* explores these fascinating members of the world of fungus. Through simple experiments you will find out what fungi like to eat, where they live, how they grow, and the important role they play in our lives.

What Makes a Fungus a Fungus?

Even though there are many different sizes, shapes, and colors of fungi, all fungi are really made up of the same parts. Most fungi start out as a *spore*, which is like a one-celled seed. If spores end up in a warm place where there is food, oxygen, and water, a thread, or *hypha*, will begin to grow out of the spore.

Hyphae (the plural of hypha) are microscopic threads that are shaped like tubes and make up the body of a fungus. These threads interweave with each other to form the *mycelium*, which looks like a delicate, lacy cobweb.

The mycelium, also called the *feeding body*, is the part of the fungus that breaks down and eats other organisms. When the mycelium is full, it creates a *fruiting body*, which is the part of a fungus that we see growing (for example, a mushroom). The fruiting body then produces millions of spores, and the cycle starts all over again as wind carries the spores off to find new food.

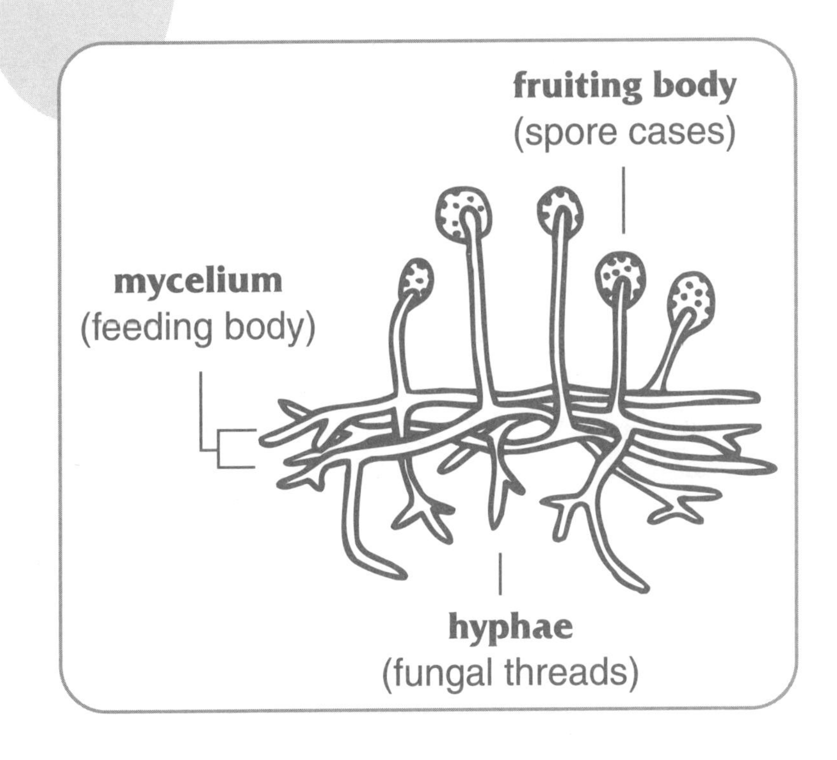

For many years, people wondered if a fungus was a plant or an animal. Fungi are like plants in some ways, but they are not true plants because they don't contain the green pigment called *chlorophyll*. Chlorophyll, along with energy from the sun, enables plants to make their own food. Fungi have to eat other plants and animals, just like people. Fungi aren't animals, however, because they can't digest food inside their bodies. Fungi are definitely in a class by themselves. To make things simple, scientists have split all life forms into five classifications, or *kingdoms*. Fungi make up one of those kingdoms. The other four are the bacteria, protist, plant, and animal kingdoms.

Fungi play a very interesting and important role in the life cycle because they recycle organic material from dead life-forms.

Fungus—Friend or Foe?

We tend to think of fungi as yucky, oozing, harmful organisms. Sometimes they are. Fungi can be very dangerous, but they are also important to the existence of other life-forms.

Fungi are extremely valuable to humans. Mushrooms are grown in enormous quantities and enjoyed in many recipes all over the world. Fungi provide vitamins and add flavor to many foods. Yeasts are important to us—without them we would have no bread. The makers of cheese add fungus molds to cheeses to give them special flavors.

Many medicines that we depend on come from fungi. Among these are *antibiotics* that kill bacteria. The most famous antibiotic, *penicillin*, is produced by a blue-green mold and was discovered in 1928. Penicillin has probably saved more lives than any other medicine.

Besides being an important source of food and medicine, fungi play an important role in the life cycle. What fungi do best is break down dead plants and animals. If there were no fungi, forests would be full of fallen trees and leaves. As fungi break down dead matter, soil becomes enriched with plant food, and valuable *carbon dioxide* (CO_2) is released into the air. This CO_2 is used by plants to make more food.

Despite the fact that fungi are essential to all living things, they can also be a nuisance. Fungi sneak into our homes when it is damp and attack our food, wood, leather, and clothing. When this happens, our food spoils, our wood rots, and *mildew*, a form of fungus, damages our clothing and upholstery. That's when "fungicides" come in handy. Fungicides are chemicals that we use to kill fungi.

Fungi can cause disease to people, animals, and crops. Sometimes these diseases cause serious illness or death. Fungi, however, do a lot more good than harm to the environment. Let's look at ways of identifying some of the many kinds of fungi that live in our world.

It's All in the Spores

There are many ways to identify fungi. One way is by examining their spores. Different fungi produce different colors and shapes of spores. Some are smooth and some are spiked. Spores are so tiny and light that the slightest breeze can blow them great distances. One way to capture fungal spores is to wait for it to rain. Rain carries spores. If you hold a petri (pee-tree) dish, like the ones included in this kit, under a gentle rain, you will definitely catch some spores. It helps to put sticky tape in the petri dish beforehand. When the dish dries, you can use your magnifying glass to identify what kind of spore you have. Here are six of the most common fungal spores:

Alternaria

Causes carrots and potatoes to rot

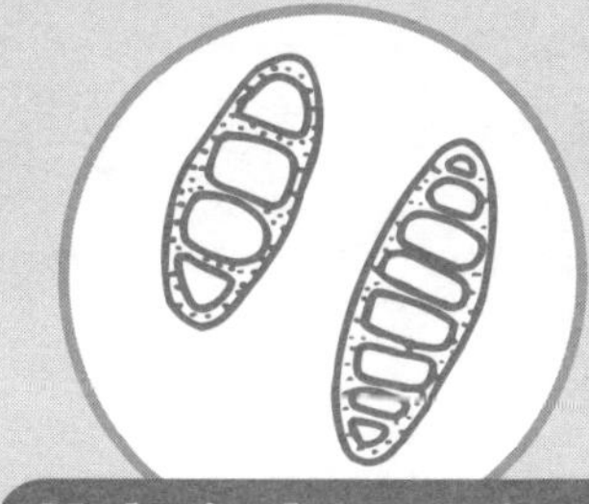

Helminthosporium

Causes oats to rot

Penicillium

A blue-green fruit mold that produces penicillin

Mushroom

The fruiting body of an underground fungus

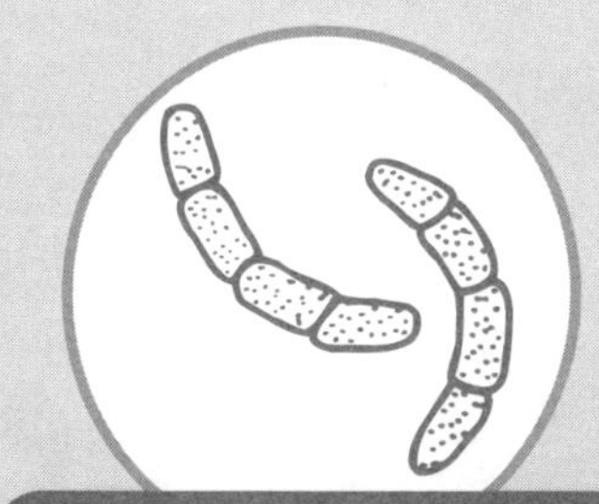

Fusarium

Causes celery to turn yellow

Aspergillus

A mold that causes bread and fruit to turn black

If Looks Could Kill

Sometimes we leave food in our kitchen just a bit too long. When we do this, fungi go to work changing it into food for themselves. Once this happens, don't eat it! To find out what kinds of fungi have moved into your refrigerator, take a closer look at them with your magnifying glass. Then match up what you see on this chart below:

	If there is:	You have this type of fungus:
1	*Fuzzy black, white, and/or gray areas, and you only see many small dots, and no hyphae*	**Aspergillus flavus** *mold on nuts and grains*
2	*Fuzzy black, white, and/or gray areas, and you can see white/gray hyphae, with no black dots*	**Mucor** *fluffy white mold on bread, fruit, and mushrooms*
	with black dots	**Rhizopus** *black bread mold*
3	*Fuzzy yellow or blue-green areas, with yellow hyphae and many dark dots*	**Aspergillus niger** *black mold on bread and fruit*
	with blue-green/gray hyphae and hardly any, or no dark dots	**Penicillium** *used to make penicillin*

EXPERIMENT #1

Spoiled Rotten Molds

When identifying fungi, it's hard not to mention *molds*. As you can see by the chart on page 6, molds are fungi that spend most of their time growing on our food. These first two experiments will let you see molds in a whole new light. *Remember: In many of the experiments, you will be growing fungus on different kinds of food. Never eat any food that has mold or any other type of fungus growing on it.*

Experiment 1: Your Everyday Bread Mold

You will need:

- *two jars with lids (each big enough to hold a slice of bread, folded)*
- *2 slices of bread*
- *a piece of cloth*
- *a rubber band*
- *water*

1. ***Slightly dampen each slice of bread. Then wipe each slice on a dusty surface, like a floor, so that some particles stick to the bread. Put one slice in a jar and put the lid on tightly (you might have to fold the bread to fit in the jar).***
2. ***Put the second slice of bread in the other jar and cover the top of the jar with the piece of cloth. Wrap the cloth tightly around the rim of the jar with the rubber band.***
3. ***Put the jars next to each other in a shady, warm place. Wait about a week. Try to guess which one will grow more mold.***

Results: The bread in the jar covered with the cloth will have a lot more dark mold on it than the bread in the jar with the tight lid. The bread in the jar with the tight lid might have fluffy white mildew on it instead of mold. The reason is because molds, like all fungi, need *oxygen* to grow. The cloth-covered jar allowed more oxygen to enter the jar, which resulted in more mold. Now let's look at a more colorful mold.

EXPERIMENT #2

Blue-Green Mold, Anyone?

One type of mold that may grow on the bread in Experiment #1 is blue-green in color, like penicillin. If you look at the spores of penicillin with a magnifying glass, you will see that they look like tiny blue brushes (*Penicillium* means "brush" in Latin). You can grow a blue-green mold on a piece of *fresh* fruit by *transferring* spores from other blue-green molds. If you can't find an old moldy orange, lemon, or bleu cheese, cut a lemon or orange in half. Then wipe one half on a dusty surface. Put it in a jar and place the jar in a shady, warm place. Wait a few days.

Experiment 2: Transferring Your Fruit and Cheese Molds

Note: You will need a grown-up helper for this experiment.

You will also need:

- *a moldy orange, lemon, bleu cheese, or the blue-green mold from the bread in Experiment #1*
- *a specimen stick (included)*
- *a fresh orange or lemon*
- *a knife*
- *a jar*

1. ***Find some blue-green mold on an old orange, lemon, bleu cheese, or the bread from Experiment #1.***
2. ***Ask an adult to cut a fresh orange or lemon in half.***
3. ***Use a specimen stick and touch some of the blue-green mold you found or grew yourself. Wipe the mold on the inside of the fresh cut orange or lemon.***
4. ***Put the fresh orange or lemon in a jar. Keep the lid loose so oxygen can get inside.***
5. ***Place the jar in a shady, warm place. Wait a few days.***

Results: When you look in the jar, you will see blue-green mold growing on the spot where you wiped the mold. The reason is simple. When spores land on a place that they like—in this case a warm, moist orange or lemon—they start growing!

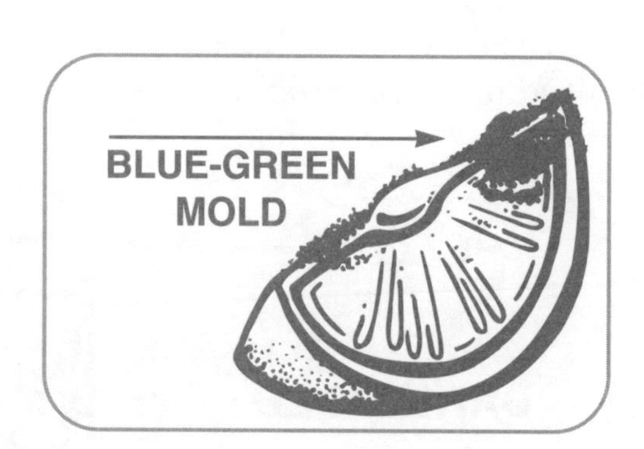

Fungi Eating Habits

The last two experiments showed you how easily fungi snatch up your food for themselves. Let's see exactly how they do that.

Because fungi are not plants, they don't contain *chlorophyll*. Therefore they can't make their own food like plants do. Instead, fungi devour anything in their path (except metal). The way fungi eat is completely different from the way we eat. We eat our solid food and then we break it down later. Fungi do the opposite. Fungi find good, solid food and break it down *first* by producing digestive chemicals, or *enzymes*. When the food is finally turned to liquidy mush, the fungi gobble it up by sucking it through the thin walls of their hyphae.

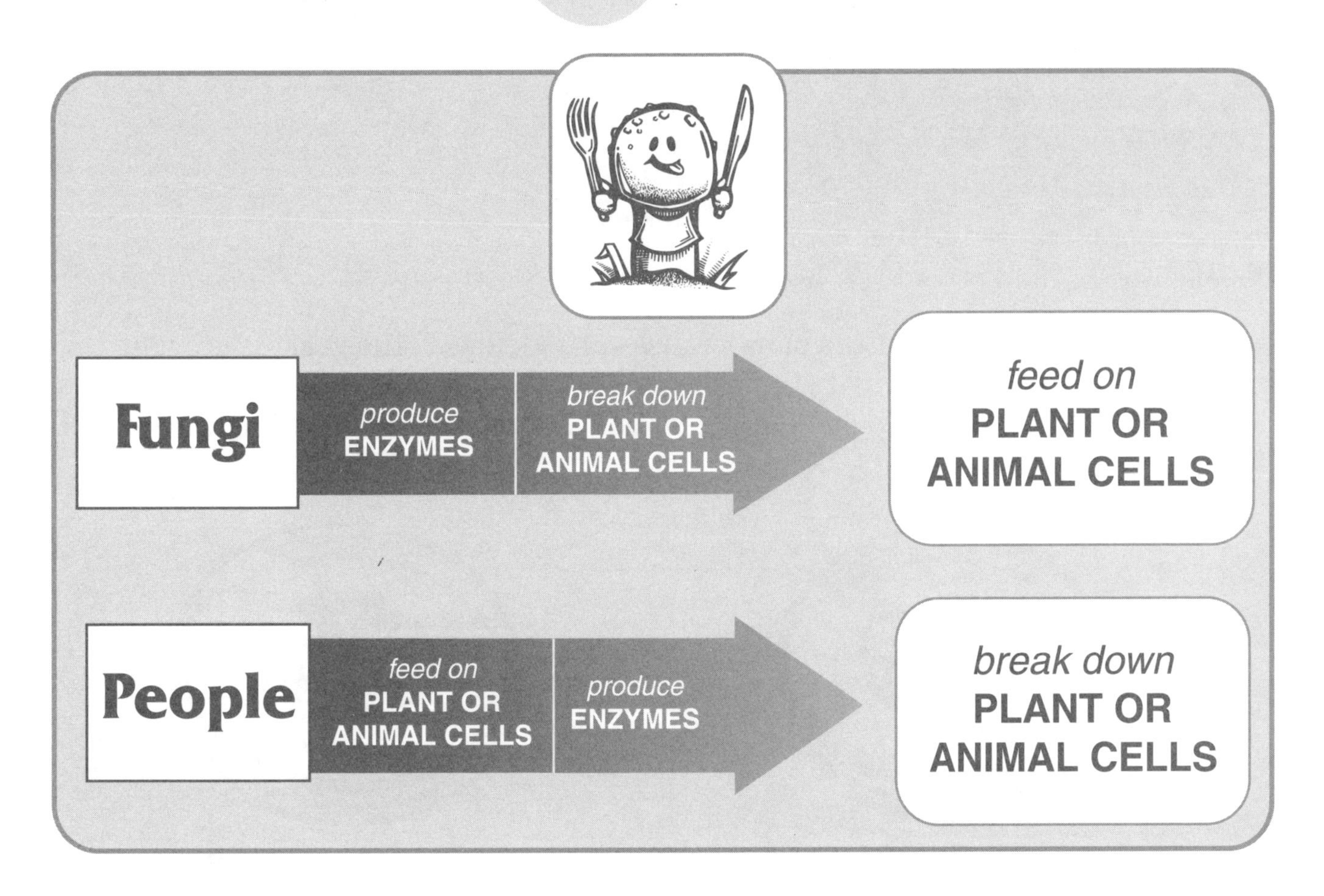

You've seen for yourself how quickly a fungus can eat. One fungus that eats extremely fast is a *yeast*. Let's take a closer look at the speedy eating habits of these tiny fungi.

EXPERIMENT #3

Amazing Yeasts

Yeasts are one-celled fungi that play a big role in the making of all our breads. If yeast is added to anything that contains sugar, it goes to work immediately, feeding on the sugar and multiplying rapidly. Let's see how fast yeast can eat a slice of banana.

Experiment 3: Feeding a banana to your yeast

You will need:

- *two petri dishes (included)*
- *yeast (included)*
- *a banana*

1. Peel the banana and break off two thin pieces.

2. Put one piece in each petri dish.

3. Sprinkle a pinch of yeast on only one of the pieces.

4. Put both lids on loosely.

5. Leave the petri dishes in a warm place for a few days.

Results: You will discover that the banana slice sprinkled with the yeast is growing fungus much faster than the other slice. The yeast is actually changing the sugar in the banana into a *gas*. The same thing happens when you use yeast to bake bread, as you will see later.

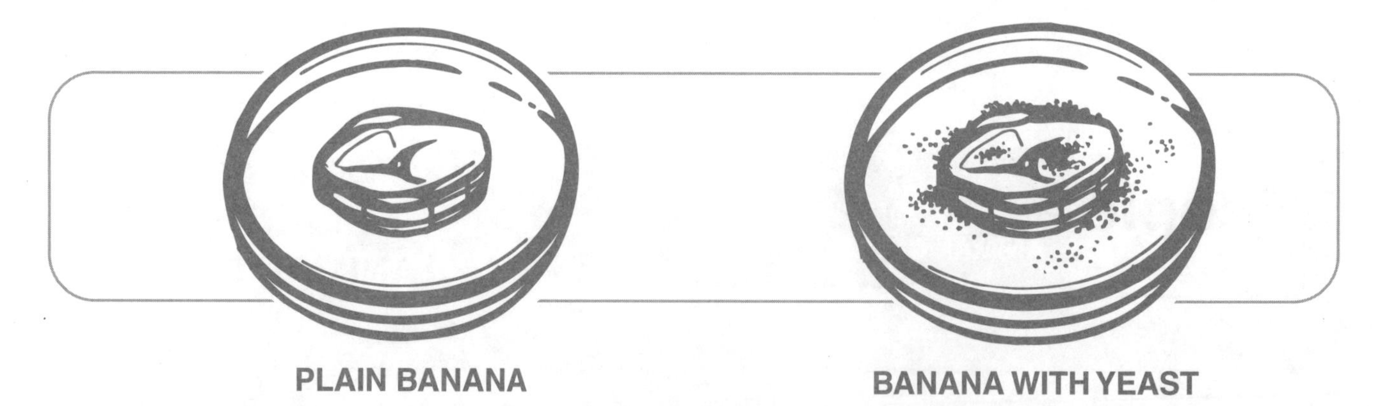

Yeasts, like all fungi, need food to grow. They can live almost anywhere, but they prefer a certain temperature. The next experiment will show you if fungi like warm or cold climates.

EXPERIMENT #4

Alaska or Hawaii?

Experiment 4: Where are fungi the happiest?

You will need:

- *four pinches of yeast (included)*
- *two teaspoons of sugar*
- *two small bottles*
- *two jars*
- *water*

1. Mix one spoonful of sugar and two pinches of yeast with water in each bottle.

2. Place each jar over a bottle as shown below. Carefully turn them upside down.

3. Put one jar in a cold place (like a refrigerator) and the other jar in a warm place. Let them sit for a few days.

Results: The yeast in the warm place grew much faster than the yeast in the cold place. Temperature means a lot to yeast and other fungi. Next you'll see that fungus is also very particular about the amount of sun it gets.

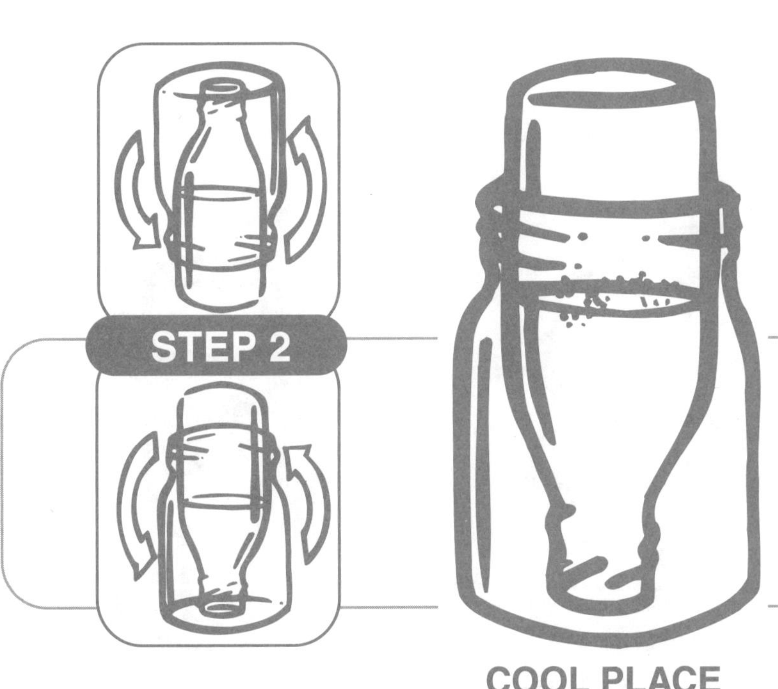

WARM PLACE

EXPERIMENT #5

Day or Night?

Besides preferring warmth over cold, yeast also prefer a certain kind of light. The next experiment will show if fungi like darkness or bright, sunny places.

Experiment 5: Do fungi like to be in the dark or the light?

You will need:

- *four pinches of yeast (included)*
- *two teaspoons of sugar*
- *two bottles*
- *two jars*
- *water*

1. Mix one spoonful of sugar and two pinches of yeast with water in each bottle.

2. Place each jar over a bottle and turn them upside down as shown below.

3. Put one jar in a sunny place (like a windowsill) and the other jar in a dark place. Let them sit for a few days.

Results: The yeast in the dark place grew much faster than the yeast in the sunny place. The reason is because ultraviolet rays from the sun kill yeast and other fungi. The next experiment will show you some other things that kill fungi.

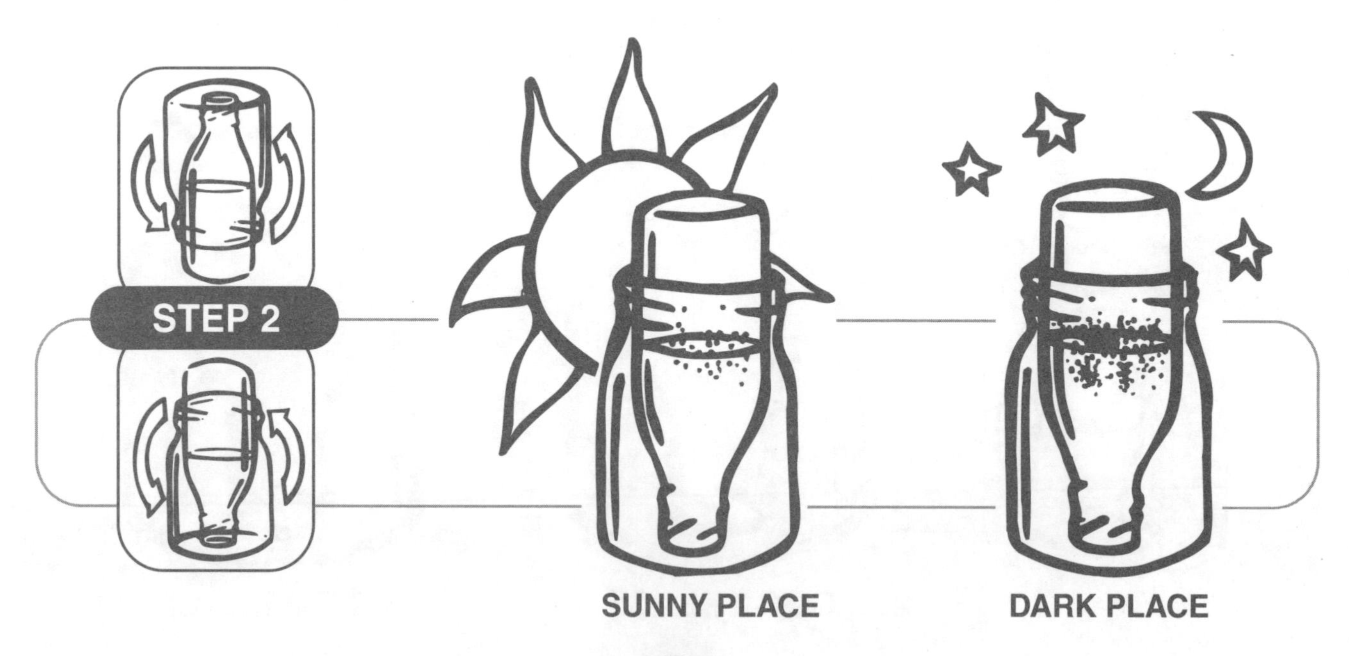

EXPERIMENT #6

Fungi Enemies

You saw that ultraviolet rays can kill yeast. If you don't want the food in your refrigerator to spoil, there are many ways to prevent fungi from growing on it. Treating foods with lemon juice, garlic, vinegar, and salt will keep fungi at a distance. Let's see how salt attacks fungi.

Experiment 6: Killer Salt

You will need:
- *two tall glasses*
- *a carrot*
- *water*
- *salt*

1. ***Snap a carrot into two 3" pieces.***
2. ***Fill each glass halfway with water.***
3. ***Pour salt into one of the glasses and stir it until it dissolves. Keep adding salt until it no longer dissolves.***
4. ***Put a piece of carrot in each glass.***
5. ***Wait a few hours.***

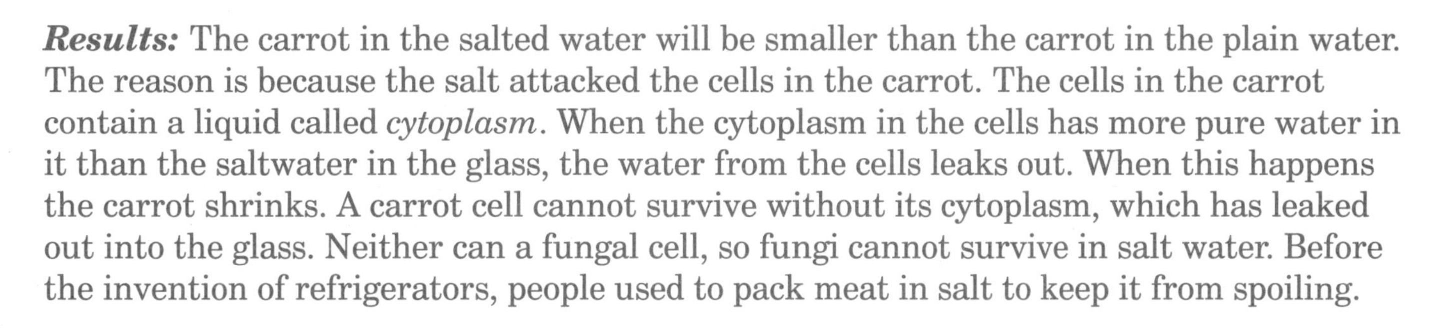

Results: The carrot in the salted water will be smaller than the carrot in the plain water. The reason is because the salt attacked the cells in the carrot. The cells in the carrot contain a liquid called *cytoplasm*. When the cytoplasm in the cells has more pure water in it than the saltwater in the glass, the water from the cells leaks out. When this happens the carrot shrinks. A carrot cell cannot survive without its cytoplasm, which has leaked out into the glass. Neither can a fungal cell, so fungi cannot survive in salt water. Before the invention of refrigerators, people used to pack meat in salt to keep it from spoiling.

As you can see, there are ways to keep fungi from destroying your food. Sometimes, though, we need fungi to help us cook our food. The next experiment will prove this.

EXPERIMENT #7

Fresh, Baked Yeast Bread

Did you know that 95% of all bread contains, you guessed it—a type of fungus? Before you yell, "Gross!" keep in mind that yeast is a fungus. Let's bake some bread, with fungi in it, for the whole family.

Experiment 7: Recipe for fungus bread

Note: You will need a grown-up helper for this experiment.

You will also need:

- *3 tablespoons butter at room temperature*
- *clean kitchen towel and oven mitt*
- *wooden spoon and cooling rack*
- *½ package of yeast (included)*
- *measuring cups and spoons*
- *small pot and loaf pan*
- *2 large mixing bowls*
- *2 teaspoons salt*
- *1 tablespoon oil*
- *3 cups of flour*
- *½ cup sugar*
- *1 cup milk*

1. ***Ask an adult to help you heat the milk in the pot on the stove over medium heat until it starts to boil. Turn off the heat, and let the milk cool for 10 minutes.***
2. ***Put the yeast, flour, sugar, and salt in the large mixing bowl and stir it with the wooden spoon. Add 2 tablespoons of butter and the milk. Stir until a thick dough starts to form. Add more flour if it isn't thick enough.***
3. ***Sprinkle some flour on a flat surface. Move the dough to the floured surface. Sprinkle more flour on the dough and knead the dough with your hands. To knead the dough, push and fold the dough for 5 minutes. Shape the dough into a ball.***
4. ***Spread the oil all over the inside of the second mixing bowl. Put the dough in the bowl. Turn the dough so that oil is also on the top of the dough. Cover the dough with a clean kitchen towel.***
5. ***Place the bowl in a warm place and let the yeast go to work. Wait an hour and you will see that the dough is twice the size it was before.***
6. ***Take the dough out of the bowl and push the air out of it. Then shape it back into a ball, put it back in the bowl, cover it with the towel, and let it rise again for about 30 minutes.***

7. Rub 1 tablespoon of butter on the bottom and sides of the loaf pan.
8. Place the dough in the loaf pan, cover the pan with the towel, and let it sit for another 30 minutes.
9. Preheat the oven to 350° F. Ask an adult to help put the loaf pan in the oven. Bake about 35 minutes.
10. Then ask an adult to remove the pan with the oven mitt and place it on the cooling rack. Let the bread cool.

Results: You will have a delicious, fluffy loaf of yeast bread. The reason the bread is so light is because the yeast reacted with the sugar to produce carbon dioxide in the dough. Remember when the yeast changed the sugar in the banana to a gas? The same process occurred here. The carbon dioxide caused the dough to rise, which created all the tiny holes and pockets in the loaf of bread. Not bad for a fungus!

By baking bread you showed how yeast breaks down sugar and turns it into gas. The next experiment will show you how much CO_2 fungi can really make.

EXPERIMENT #8

CO_2 and You

Yeast and other fungi use oxygen, warm air, and moisture to create carbon dioxide gas. This experiment will show you how to create your own bottle full of CO_2.

Experiment 8: Make a bottle of CO_2

You will need:

- *a thin bottle with a cap*
- *yeast (included)*
- *½ cup sugar*
- *a wide jar and warm water*

1. **Pour the sugar in the bottle. Mix it with a few pinches of yeast.**
2. **Pour warm water in the bottle until it is halfway full.**
3. **Stir the liquid well and then fill the bottle up all the way.**
4. **Place the bottle in a warm, dark place. Put the jar over the top of the bottle as shown below. Hold the jar tightly against the bottle and flip them both over. Make sure the water doesn't leak out of the bottle.**
5. **Wait 3-4 hours. Gas will start forming at the top of the bottle, which will push the water out of the bottle. In a few days, the bottle will be completely filled with carbon dioxide gas.**
6. **Drain the water out of the jar by holding the bottle tightly against the jar and tilting them both over a sink. When the jar is empty, turn the bottle and jar back over. Pull the jar off the bottle and put the cap on the bottle.**

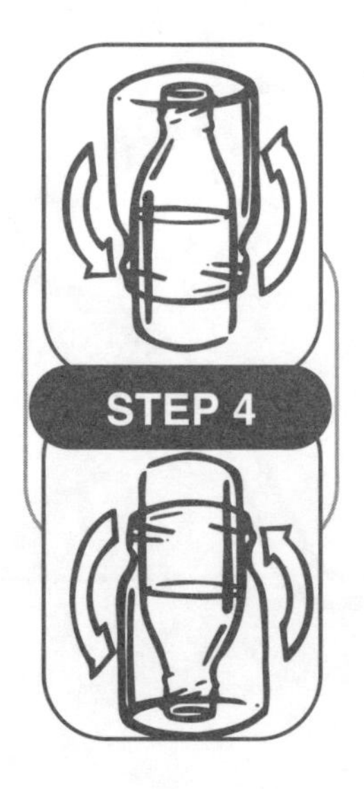

Results: You now have a bottle of carbon dioxide gas! If you don't believe it, move on to the next experiment.

AFTER A FEW DAYS

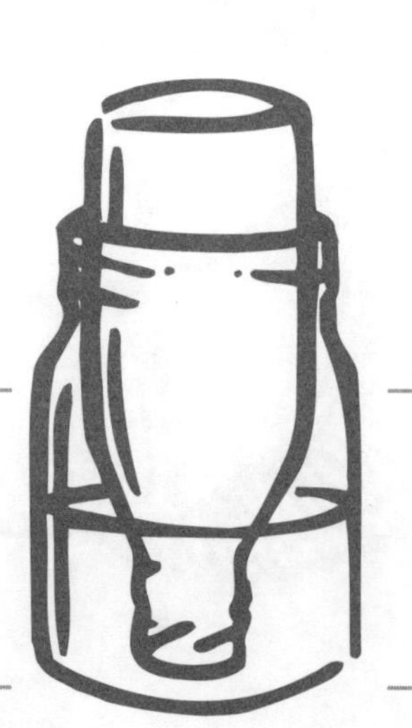

TWIST CAP ON BOTTLE

EXPERIMENT #9

CO_2 and Fungus – Good Roommates?

A way of proving that the bottle in the last experiment is really filled with carbon dioxide is to try to grow mold inside of it.

Experiment 9: Will fungus grow in a bottle of CO_2 ?

You will need:

- *the bottle filled with gas from the last experiment*
- *two small pieces of bread*
- *water*
- *a jar*

1. Sprinkle water on two small pieces of bread.

2. Put one slice in a jar with a loose lid.

3. Put the other slice of bread in the bottle of carbon dioxide and put the cap on the bottle.

4. Put the jar and the bottle in a warm, dark place for a day or two.

Results: You'll find that mold grew on the slice of bread in the jar. The bread in the bottle will have no mold on it. As you know, to break down the bread, the mold needs oxygen. This proves that the bottle from the last experiment is filled with carbon dioxide.

You've seen how fungi grow, what kind of environment makes them happiest, and how to kill them. You've learned all about molds and yeast. But what about the most popular fungi of all? The fungi we eat on our pizzas and in our salads. We're talking about the amazing edible fungus—the mushroom.

EXPERIMENT #10

What Exactly Is a Mushroom?

Earlier we learned that a mushroom is a fruiting body of a fungus. It's what pops up after the mycelium of the fungus is full from eating another organism. The parts of a mushroom include the umbrella-shaped *cap*, the *stem*, and the *gills* which are under the cap and look like the pages in a book. Mushroom *spores*, which are like seeds, grow from the gills. As the gills open, the spores fall to the ground. The spores send out the threads called *hyphae*. As you learned earlier, bunches of hyphae meshed together form the cobweb-like *mycelium*.

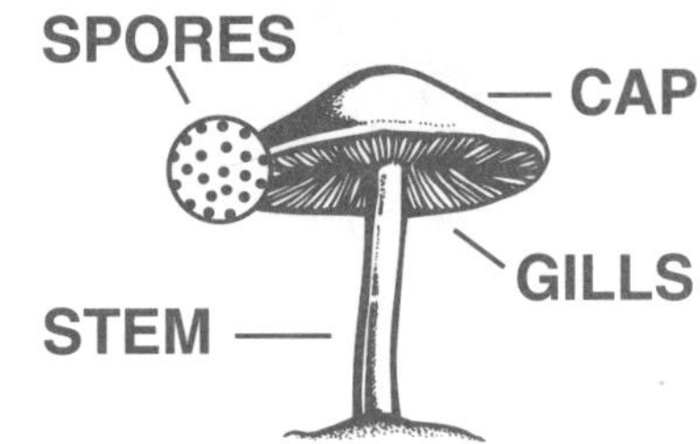

As you know, spores are very tiny. You can't even see them without a magnifying glass. But this experiment will allow you to see lots of spores together.

Experiment 10: Mushroom Spore Prints

You will need:

- *a ripe mushroom, bought from a supermarket, with the gills showing*
- *a piece of white paper*
- *a glass*

1. Snap the stem off the mushroom.

2. Lay the cap down on the paper, so that the gills face down.

3. Cover the mushroom cap with the glass to keep the spores from blowing away.

4. Wait a day.

Results: You should have a print like this one. The spores should be very easy to see now.

Mushrooms are a popular part of our meals. They are grown in huge quantities for us to eat. For many years, however, no one knew exactly where mushrooms came from. People made up some pretty interesting stories about these beautiful fungi.

Mushroom Mania

For thousands of years, people have wondered about the origin of the mushroom. Some believed that mushrooms were umbrellas for fairies. Others thought that mushrooms were formed where lightning hit the ground. Toadstools got their name because people believed that toads used them to sit on.

Fairy Rings

In ancient times, people often wondered why mushrooms would sometimes grow in perfect circles. They called these strange circles of mushrooms "fairy rings." They believed that fairies danced around in circles at night and used the mushrooms as stools to rest on. The real explanation, however, is very simple. Sometimes the underground mycelium grows outward in all directions from a central point. When mushrooms grow from the ends of the mycelium, they form a circle. These circles of mushrooms are still called "fairy rings" today. Fairy rings grow bigger and bigger as the mycelium keeps spreading outward. Some are hundreds of years old.

Many kinds of fungi are known to grow in some not-so-normal ways, as you will see next.

The Weird Fungus Among Us

Like any other life-form, the fungus kingdom has some strange members. Below are just a few. *Remember: Not all mushrooms are edible. In fact, some are very poisonous. You should never touch, pick, or eat any type of fungus growing in the wild.*

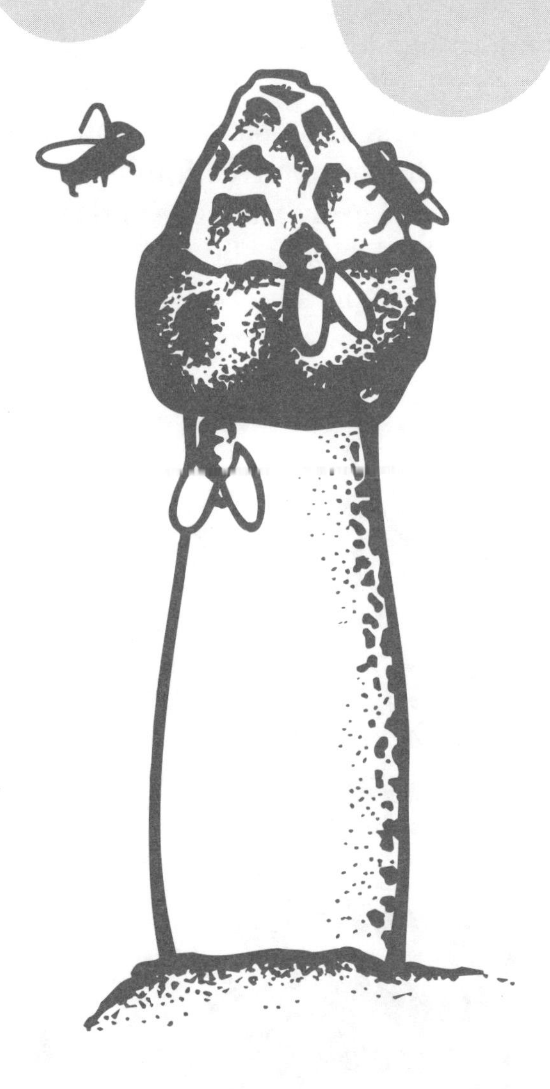

Stinkhorns: The cap of this fungus is covered with a dark, foul-smelling jelly. When flies smell stinkhorns, they fly over and eat the jelly. When the flies are finished eating, they fly away, spreading the spores so that more smelly stinkhorns can grow.

Fly Agaric: Though they look nice, these bright red mushrooms are very poisonous. These dangerous fungi grow under pine trees.

Puffballs: These are probably the biggest fungi in the world. Puffballs are usually the size of a football, but they've been known to grow ten times that size. These giant, edible fungi are usually cut in slices, breaded, and fried.

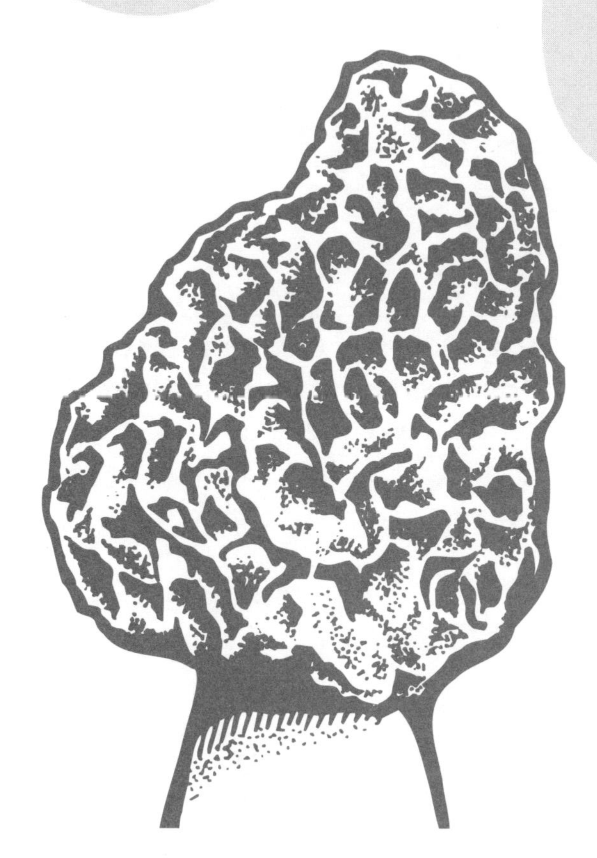

Morel Fungi: Morels are edible and grow in grassy meadows. They are a delicious, popular food in Central Europe. Morels are usually served in a cream sauce.

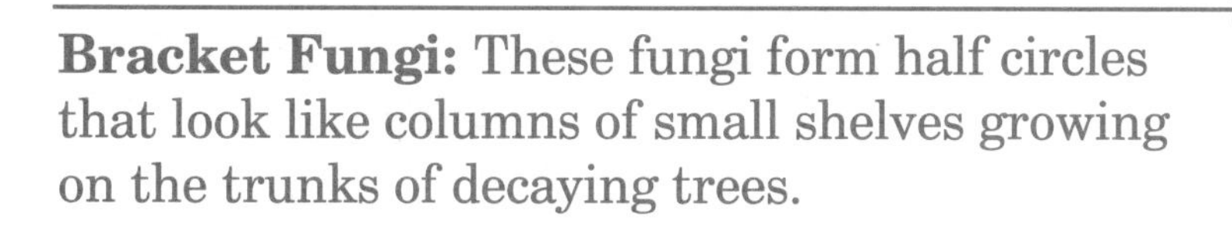

Bracket Fungi: These fungi form half circles that look like columns of small shelves growing on the trunks of decaying trees.

Earth Star: You'll find these pretty fungi growing under trees. They start out looking like onions, but then the outer layers peel back and form star shapes.

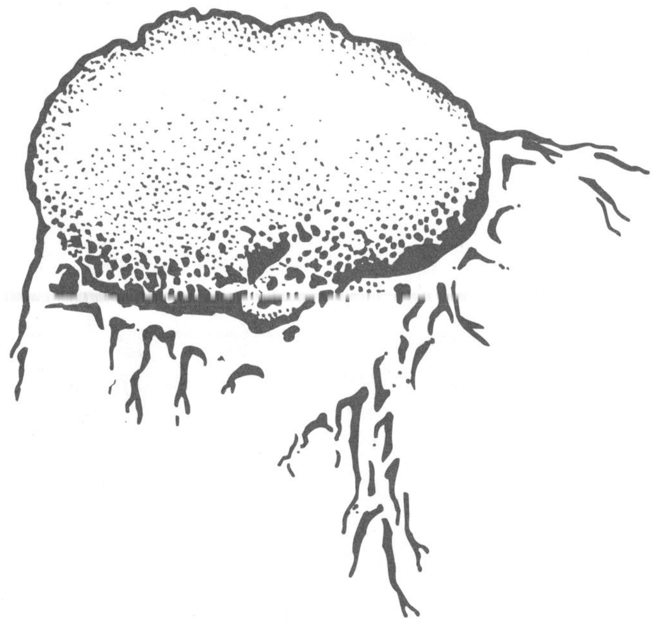

Slime Fungi: These fungi have no cap or stem and they feed on old stumps and grass. Their shapes change as they grow and spread out. Slime fungi look like soft, wet blobs.

Mildew: White, powdery mildew grows on roses and the leaves of various trees. This fluffy fungus is very common in gardens.

Now you'll see what happens when a bunch of different fungi end up together!

The Ultimate Fungus Get-Together

When you make a *compost,* everyone's invited! Everyone who is a fungus, that is. Gardeners use a compost pile, which is basically a pile of rotting plants, to fertilize their other plants. Compost can be mixed with soil to make it rich and healthy. As you can probably imagine, compost is a perfect home for all kinds of fungi.

Making a compost pile is an on-going project. All you need is a box, barrel, or garbage pail in which to store the compost. Make sure the walls of the container have holes in them to allow air inside. Remember, fungi need air to grow. Then follow these easy instructions and be patient. A good compost pile takes about six months to become fertilizer.

1. ***After you find a suitable container for your compost, find a place far enough away from your house to keep it, preferably at the far end of your backyard. If you can't make a compost pile at home, ask your teacher if you can make one at school as a science project.***

2. ***Layer dead plants, grass clippings, leaves, sawdust, coffee grounds, and leftover fruits and vegetables in the container. After you add each layer, sprinkle water and soil. This will encourage the growth of fungi and speed up the decay.***

3. ***Study your compost pile regularly. You may see mushrooms and slime growing on top from time to time. How many different types of fungi can you identify?***

When your compost finally becomes rich fertilizer, use it in your garden to keep your plants healthy and happy. This is just one more way that fungi help make our lives a bit better.

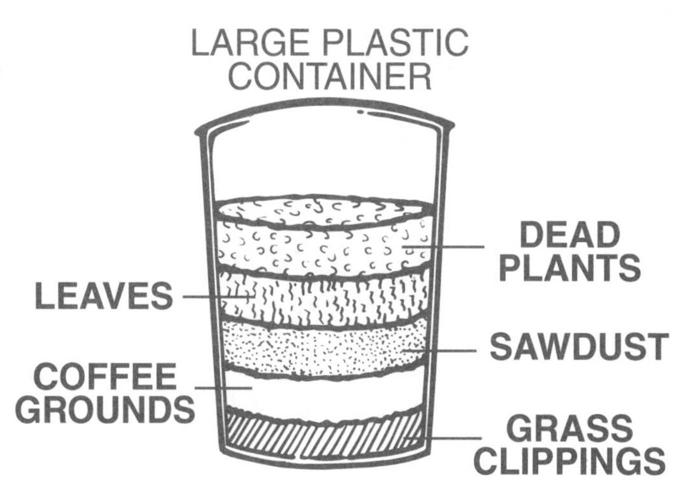

Fungus Finale

If you want to further explore the world of fungus, you won't have to go very far. Most fungi live in the soil and on the dead rotting remains of plants. Some fungi live underwater, and some even live in our homes. It's easy to set out on your own "Fungi Safari." Here are some helpful tips:

1. Never touch, pick, or eat any type of fungus you find in the wild.

2. Keep a notebook to record all the types of fungi you find. Write down the date, where you found your fungi, and what the weather was like.

3. Write down the shapes and colors of all the fungi you find.

4. Draw pictures of the fungi you find. Then you can research them to find out what kind they are.

5. Remember, part of the word "fungus" is "fun," so enjoy yourself!